EVERY BOY'S LIBRARY

THE BIOGRAPHY OF A GRIZZLY
and
75 Drawings
by
ERNEST THOMPSON SETON

Author of
The Trail of the Sandhill Stag
Wild Animals I Have Known
Art Anatomy of Animals
Mammals of Manitoba
Birds of Manitoba

Published by Grosset & Dunlap, New York

This Book is dedicated to the memory of the days spent at the Palette Ranch on the Gray-bull, where from hunter, miner, personal experience, and the host himself, I gathered many chapters of the History of Wahb.

In this Book the designs for title-page, cover, and general makeup, were done by Mrs. Grace Gallatin Thompson Seton.

List of Full-Page Drawings

They all Rushed Under it like a Lot
of Little Pigs 14
Like Children Playing 'Hands'. .
.... 18
He Stayed in the Tree till near Morning ....
32
A Savage Bobcat . . . Warned Him to
go Back.. 44
Wahb Yelled and Jerked Back 50

He Struck one Fearful, Crushing Blow 74

Ain't He an Awful Size, Though? 90

Wahb Smashed His Skull .... 102 Causing the Pool to Overflow .... .113

He Deliberately Stood up on the Pine Root 142

The Roachback Fled into the Woods............................... 150

He Paused a Moment at the Gate 165

PART I
THE CUBHOOD OF WAHB

was born over a score of years ago, away up in the wildest part of the wild West, on the head of the Little Piney, above where the Palette Ranch is now.

His Mother was just an ordinary Silvertip, living the quiet life that all Bears prefer, minding her own business and doing her duty by her family, asking no favors of any one excepting to let her alone.

It was July before she took her remarkable family down the Little Piney to the Graybull, and showed them what strawberries were, and where to find them.

Notwithstanding their Mother's deep conviction, the cubs were not remarkably big or bright; yet they were a remarkable family, for there were four of them, and it is not often a Grizzly Mother can boast of more than two.

The woolly-coated little creatures were having a fine time, and reveled in the lovely mountain summer and the abundance of good things. Their Mother turned over each log and flat stone they came to, and the moment it was lifted they all rushed under it like a lot

"THEY ALL RUSHED UNDER IT LIKE A LOT OF LITTLE PIGS.'

of little pigs to lick up the ants and grubs there hidden.

It never once occurred to them that Mammy's strength might fail sometime, and let the great rock drop just as they got under it; nor would any one have thought so that might have Chanced to see that huge arm and that shoulder sliding about under the great yellow robe she wore. No, no; that arm could never fail. The little ones were quite right. So they hustled and tumbled one another at each fresh log in their haste to be first, and squealed little squeals, and growled little growls, as if each was a pig, a pup, and a kitten all rolled into one.

They were well acquainted with the common little brown ants that harbor under logs in the uplands, but now they came for the first time on one of the hills of the great, fat, luscious Wood-ant, and they all crowded around to lick up those that ran out. But they soon found that they were licking up more cactus-prickles and sand than ants, till their Mother said in Grizzly, " Let me show you how."

She knocked off the top of the hill, then laid her great paw flat on it for a few moments, and as the angry ants swarmed on to it she licked them up with one lick, and got a good rich mouthful to crunch, without a grain of sand or a cactus-stinger in it. The cubs soon learned. Each put up both his little brown paws, so that there was a ring of paws all around the ant-hill, and

"LIKE CHILDREN PLAYING 'HANDS.'"

there they sat, like children playing hands and each licked first the right and then the left paw, or one cuffed his brother's ears for licking a paw that was not his own, till the ant-hill was cleared out and they were ready for a change.

Ants are sour food and made the Bears thirsty, so the old one led down to the river. After they had drunk as much as they wanted, and dabbled their feet, they walked down the bank to a pool, where the old one's keen eye caught sight of a number of Buffalo-fish basking on the bottom. The water was very low, mere pebbly rapids between these deep holes, so Mammy said to the little ones:

" Now you all sit there on the bank and learn something new."

First she went to the lower end

of the pool and stirred up a cloud of mud which hung in the still water, and sent a long tail floating like a curtain over the rapids just below. Then she went quietly round by land, and sprang into the upper end of the pool with all the noise she could. The fish had crowded to that end, but this sudden attack sent them off in a panic, and they dashed blindly into the mud-cloud. Out of fifty fish there is always a good chance of some being fools, and half a dozen of these dashed through the darkened water into the current, and before they knew it they were struggling over the shingly shallow. The old Grizzly jerked them out to the bank, and the little ones rushed noisily on these funny, short snakes that could not get away, and gobbled and gorged till their little bellies looked like balloons.

They had eaten so much now, and the sun was so hot, that all were quite sleepy. So the Mother-bear led them to a quiet little nook, and as soon as she lay down, though they were puffing with heat, they all snuggled around her and went to sleep, with their little brown paws curled in, and their little black noses tucked into their wool as though it were a very cold day.

After an hour or two they began to yawn and stretch themselves, except little Fuzz, the smallest; she poked out her sharp nose for a moment, then snuggled back be-

tween her Mother's great arms, for she was a gentle, petted little thing. The largest, the one afterward known as Wahb, sprawled over on his back and began to worry a root that stuck up, grumbling to himself as he chewed it, or slapped it with his paw for not staying where he wanted it. Presently Mooney, the mischief, began tugging at Frizzle's ears, and got his own well boxed. They clenched for a tussle; then, locked in a tight, little grizzly yellow ball, they sprawled over and over on th e grass, and, before they knew it, down a bank, and away out of sight toward the river.

Almost immediately there was an outcry of yells for help from the

little wrestlers. There could be no mistaking the real terror in their voices. Some dreadful danger was threatening.

Up jumped the gentle Mother, changed into a perfect demon, and over the bank in time to see a huge Range-bull make a deadly charge at what he doubtless took for a yellow dog. In a moment all would have been over with Frizzle, for he had missed his footing on the bank; but there was a thumping of heavy feet, a roar that startled even the great Bull, and, like a huge bounding ball of yellow fur, Mother Grizzly was upon him. Him! the monarch of the herd, the master of all these plains, what had he to fear? He bellowed his deep war-cry, and

charged to pin the old one to the bank; but as he bent to tear her with his shining horns, she dealt him a stunning blow, and before he could recover she was on his shoulders, raking the flesh from his ribs with sweep after sweep of her terrific claws.

The Bull roared with rage, and plunged and reared, dragging Mother Grizzly with him; then, as he hurled heavily off the slope> she let go to save herself, and the Bull rolled down into the river.

This was a lucky thing for him, for the Grizzly did not want to follow him there; so he waded out on the other side, and bellowing with fury and pain, slunk off to join the herd to which he belonged.

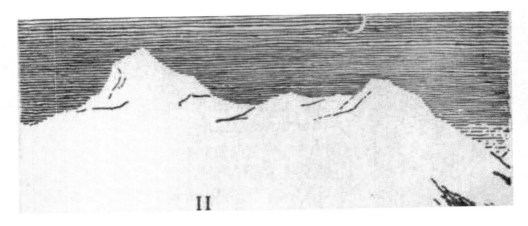

II

O D Colonel Pickett, the cattle king, was out riding the range. The night before, he had seen the new-moon descending over the white cone of Pickett's Peak.

" I saw the last moon over Frank's Peak," said he, " and the luck was against me for a month; now I reckon it's my turn."

Next morning his luck began. A letter came from Washington

granting bis request that a post-office be established at his ranch, and contained the polite inquiry, "What name do you suggest for the new post-office?"

The Colonel took down his new rifle, a 45-90 repeater. " May as well," he said; "this is my month "; and he rode up the Graybull to see how the cattle were doing. , As he passed underthe Rimrock Mountain he heard a far-away roaring as of Bulls fighting, but thought nothing of it till he rounded the point and saw on the flat below a lot of his cattle pawing the dust and bellowing as they always do when they smell the blood of one of their number. He soon saw that the great Bull, * the boss of the bunch.*

was covered with blood. His back and sides were torn as by a Mountain-lion, and his head was battered as by another Bull.

" Grizzly/' growled the Colonel, for he knew the mountains. He quickly noted the general direction of the Bull's back trail, then rode toward a high bank that offered a view. This was across the gravelly ford of the Graybull, near the mouth of the Piney. His horse splashed through the cold water and began jerkily to climb the other bank.

As soon as the rider's head rose above the bank his hand grabbed the rifle, for there in full sight were five Grizzly Bears, an old one and four cubs.

" Run for the woods, Tt growled the Mother Grizzly, for she knew that men carried guns. Not that she feared for herself; but the idea of such things among her darlings was too horrible to think of. She set off to guide them to the timber-tangle on the Lower Piney. But an awful, murderous fusillade be-gan.

and Mother Grizzly felt a deadly pang.

Rang! and poor little Fuzz rolled over with a scream of pain and lay still.

With a roar of hate and fury Mother Grizzly turned to attack the enemy.

Bang! and she fell paralyzed and dying with a high shoulder

shot. And the three little cubs, not knowing what to do, ran back to their Mother.

Bang! bang! and Mooney and Frizzle sank in dying agonies beside her, and Wahb, terrified and stupefied, ran in a circle about them. Then, hardly knowing why, he turned and dashed into the timber-tangle, and disappeared as a last bang left him with a stinging pain and a useless, broken hind paw.

THAT is why the post-office was called Four-Bears. The Colonel seemed pleased with what he had done; indeed, he told of it himself.

But away up in the woods of Anderson's Peak that night a little

lame Grizzly might have been seen wandering, limping along, leaving a bloody spot each time he tried to set down his hind paw; whining and whimpering, " Mother! Mother! Oh, Mother, where are you?" for he was cold and hungry, and had such a pain in his foot. But there was no Mother to come to him, and he dared not go back where he had left her, so he wandered aimlessly about among the pines.

Then he smelled some strange animal smell and heard heavy footsteps; and not knowing what else to do, he climbed a tree. Presently a band of great, long-necked, slim-legged animals, taljer than his Mother, came by under the tree. He

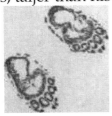

'HE STAYED IN THE TREE TILL NEAR MORNING.

had seen such once before and had not been afraid of them then, because he had been with his Mother. But now he kept very quiet in the tree, and the big creatures stopped picking the grass when they were near him, and blowing their noses, ran out of sight.

He stayed in the tree till near morning, and then he was so sti with cold that he could scarcely get down. But the warm sun came up, and he felt better as he sought about for berries and ants, for he was very hungry. Then he went back to the Piney and put his wounded foot in the ice-cold water.

He wanted to get back to the mountains again, but still he felt he must go to where he had left his

Mother and brothers. When the afternoon grew warm, he went limping down the stream through the timber, and down on the banks of the Graybull till he came to the place where yesterday they had had the fish-feast; and he eagerly crunched the heads and remains that he found. But there was an odd and horrid smell on the wind. It frightened him, and as he went down to where he last had seen his Mother the smell grew worse. He peeped out cautiously at the place, and saw there a lot of Coyotes, tearing at something. What it was he did not know; but he saw no Mother, and the smell that sickened and terrified him was worse than ever, so he quietly turned back toward the timber-tangle of the Lower Piney, and nevermore came back to look for his lost family. He wanted his Mother as much as ever, but something told him it was no use.

As cold night came down, he missed her more and more again, and he whimpered as he limped along, a miserable, lonely, little, motherless Bear—not lost in the mountains, for he had no home to seek, but so sick and lonely, and with such a pain in his foot, and in his stomach a craving for the drink that would nevermore be his. That night he found a hollow log, and crawling in, he tried to dream that his Mother's great, furry arms were around him, and he snuffled himself to sleep.

AHB had always been a gloomy little Bear; and the string of misfortunes that came on him just as his mind was forming made him more than ever sullen and morose. It seemed as though every one were against him. Hetriedto keep out of sight in the upper woods of the Piney, seeking his food by day and resting at night in the hollow log. But one evening he found it occupied by a Porcupine as big as
himself and as bad as a cactus-bush. Wahb could do nothing with him. He had to give up the log and seek another nest.

One day he went down on the Graybull flat to dig some roots that his Mother had taught him were good. But before he had well begun, a grayish-looking animal came out of a hole in the ground and rushed at him, hissing and growling. Wahb did not know it was a Badger, but he saw it was a fierce animal as big as himself. He was sick, and lame too, so he limped away and never stopped till he was on a ridge in the next canon. Here a Coyote saw him, and came bounding after him, calling at the same time to another to come and join the fun. Wahb was near a tree, so

\ m

he scrambled up to the branches. The Coyotes came bounding and yelping below, but their noses told them that this was a young Grizzly they had chased, and they soon decided that a young Grizzly in a tree means a Mother Grizzly not far away, and they had better let him alone.

After they had sneaked off Wahb came down and returned to the Piney. There was better feeding on the Graybull, but every one seemed against him there now that his loving guardian was gone, while on the Piney he had peace at least sometimes, and there were plenty of trees that he could climb when an enemy came.

His broken foot was a long time in healing; indeed, it never got quite well. The wound healed and the soreness wore off, but it left a stiffness that gave him a slight limp, and the sole-balls grew together quite unlike those of the other foot. It particularly annoyed him when he had to climb a tree or run fast from his enemies; and of them he found no end, though never once did a friend cross his path. When he lost his Mother he lost his best and only friend. She would have taught him much that he had to learn by bitter experience, and would have saved him from most of the ills that befell him in his cubhood—ills so many and so dire that but for his native sturdiness he never could have passed through alive.

The pinons bore plentifully that year, and the winds began to shower down the ripe, rich nuts. Life was becoming a little easier for Wahb. He was gaining in health and strength, and the creatures he daily met now let him alone. But as he feasted on the pinons one morning after a gale, a great Black-bear came marching down the hill. * No one meets a friend in the woods/ was a byword that Wahb had learned already. H e swung up the nearest tree. Atfirstthe Black-bear was scared, for he smelled the smell of Grizzly; but when he saw it was only a cub, he took courage and came growling at Wahb. He could climb as well as the little Grizzly, or better, and high as Wahb went, the Blackbear fol-

lowed, and when Wahb got out on the smallest and highest twig that would carry him, the Blackbear cruelly shook him off, so that he was thrown to the ground, bruised and shaken and half-stunned. He limped away moaning, and the only thing that kept the Blackbear from following him up and perhaps killing him was the fear that the old Grizzly might be about. So Wahb was driven away down the creek from all the good pinon woods.

There was not much food on the Graybull now. The berries were nearly all gone; there were no fish or ants to get, and Wahb, hurt, lonely, and miserable, wandered on and on, till he was away down toward the Meteetsee.

A Coyote came bounding and barking through the sage-brush after him. Wahb tried to run, but it was no use; the Coyote was soon up with him. Then with a sudden rush of desperate courage Wahb turned and charged his foe. The astonished Coyote gave a scared yowl or two, and fled with his tail between his legs. Thus Wahb learned that war is the price of peace.

But the forage was poor here; there were too many cattle; and Wahb was making for a far-away pifion woods in the Meteetsee Canon when he saw a man, just like the one he had seen on that day of sorrow. At the same moment he heard a bang, and some

'A SAVAGE BOBCAT . . . WARNED HIM TO GO BACK.'

sage-brush rattled and fell just over his back. All the dreadful smells and dangers of that day came back to his memory, and Wahb ran as he never had run before.

He soon got into a gully and followed it into the canon. An opening between two cliffs seemed to offer shelter, but as he ran toward it a Range-cow came trotting between, shaking her head at him and snorting threats against his life.

He leaped aside upon a long log that led up a bank, but at once a savage Bobcat appeared on the other end and warned him to go back. It was no time to quarrel. Bitterly Wahb felt that the world was full of enemies. But he turned

and scrambled up a rocky bank into the pirion woods that border the benches of the Meteetsee.

The Pine Squirrels seemed to resent his coming, and barked furiously. They were thinking about their pifion-nuts. They knew that this Bear was coming to steal their provisions, and they followed him overhead to scold and abuse him, with such an outcry that an enemy might have followed him by their noise, which was exactly what they intended.

There was no one following, but it made Wahb uneasy and nervous. So he kept on till he reached the timber line, where both food and foes were scarce, and here on the edge of the Mountain-sheep land v at last he got a chance to rest.

K

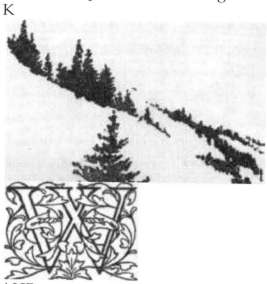

AHB never was
sweet-tempered like his baby sister, and the persecutions by his numerous foes were making him more and more sour. Why could not they let him alone in his misery? Why was every one against him? If only he had his Mother back! If he could only have killed that Black-bear that had driven him from his woods! It did not occur to him that some day he himself would be
big. And that spiteful Bobcat, that took advantage of him; and the man that had tried to kill him. He did not forget any of them, and he hated them all.

Wahb found his new range fairly good, because it was a good nut year. He learned just what the Squirrels feared he would, for his nose directed him to the little granaries where they had stored up great quantities of nuts for winter's use. It was hard on the Squirrels, but it was good luck for Wahb, for the nuts were delicious food. And when the days shortened and the nights began to be frosty, he had grown fat and well-favored.

He traveled over all parts of the canon now, living mostly in the

higher woods, but coming down at times to forage almost as far as the river. One night as he wandered by the deep water a peculiar smell reached his nose. It was quite pleasant, so he followed it up to the water's edge. It seemed to come from a sunken log. As he reached over toward this, there was a sudden clank, and one of his paws was caught in a strong, steel Beaver-trap.

Wahb yelled and jerked back with all his strength, and tore up the stake that held the trap. He tried to shake it off, then ran away through the bushes trailing it. He tore at it with his teeth; but there it hung, quiet, cold, strong, and immovable. Every little while he

tore at it with his teeth and claws, or beat it against the ground. He buried it in the earth, then climbed a low tree, hoping to leave it behind; but still it clung, biting into his flesh. He made for his own woods, and sat down to try to puzzle it out. He did not know what it was, but his little green-brown eyes glared with a mixture of pain, fright, and fury as he tried to understand his new enemy.

He lay down under the bushes, and, intent on deliberately crush ing the thing, he held it down with one paw while he tightened his teeth on the other end, and bearing down as it slid away, the trap jaws opened and the foot was free. It was mere chance, of course, that led him to squeeze both springs at once. He did not understand it, but he did not forget it, and he got these not very clear ideas: * There is a dreadful little enemy that hides by the water and waits for one. It has an odd smell. It bites one's paws and is too hard for one to bite. But it can be got off by hard squeezing.'

For a week or more the little Grizzly had another sore paw, but it was not very bad if he did not do any climbing.

It was now the season when the Elk were bugling on the mountains. Wahb heard them all night, and once or twice had to climb to get away from one of the big-antlered Bulls. It was also the season when the trappers were coming into the

mountains, and the Wild Geese were honking overhead. There were several quite new smells in the woods, too. Wahb followed one of these up, and it led to a place where were some small logs piled together; then, mixed with the smell that had drawn him, was one that he hated — he remembered it from the time when he had lost his Mother. He sniffed about carefully, for it was not very strong, and learned that this hateful smell was on a log in front, and the sweet smell that made his mouth water was under some brush behind. So he went around, pulled away the brush till he got the prize, a piece of meat, and as he grabbed it, the log in front went down with a heavy chock.

It made Wahb jump; but he got away all right with the meat and some new ideas, and with one old idea made stronger, and that was, ' When that hateful smell is around it always means trouble.'

As the weather grew colder, Wahb became very sleepy; he slept all day when it was frosty. He had not any fixed place to sleep in; he knew a number of dry ledges for sunny weather, and one or two sheltered nooks for stormy days. He had a very comfortable nest under a root, and one day, as it began to blow and snow, he crawled into this and curled up to sleep. The storm howled without. The snow fell deeper and deeper. It draped the pine-trees till they bowed, then shook themselves clearto be draped

anew.

It drifted over the mountains and poured down the funnel-like ravines, blowing off the peaks and ridges, and filling up the hollows level with their rims It piled up over Wahb's den, shutting out the cold of the winter, shutting out itself: and Wahb slept and slept.

'E slept all winter without waking, for such is the way of Bears, and yet when spring came and aroused him, he knew that he had been asleep a long time. He was not much changed — he had grown in height, and yet was but little thinner. He was now very hungry, and forcing his way through the deep drift that still lay over his den, he set out to look for food.

There were no pinon-nuts to get, and no berries or ants; but Wahb's nose led him away up the canon to the body of a winter-killed Elk, where he had a fine feast, and then buried the rest for future use.

Day after day he came back till he had finished it. Food was very scarce for a couple of months, and after the Elk was eaten, Wahb lost all the fat he had when he awoke. One day he climbed over the Divide into the Warhouse Valley. It was warm and sunny there, vegetation was well advanced, and he found good forage. He wandered down toward the thick timber, and soon smelled the smell of another Grizzly. This grew stronger and led him to a single tree by a Bear-trail. Wahb reared up on his hind

feet to smell this tree. Itwasstrong of Bear, and was plastered with mud and Grizzly hair far higher than he could reach; and Wahb knew that it must have been a very large Bear that had rubbed himself there. He felt uneasy. He used to long to meet one of his own kind, yet now that there was a chance of it he was filled with dread.

No one had shown him anything but hatred in his lonely, unprotected life, and he could not tell what this older Bear might do. As he stood in doubt, he caught sight of the old Grizzly himself slouching along a hillside, stopping from time to time to dig up the quamash-roots and wild turnips.

He was a monster. Wahbinstinc-

tively distrusted him, and sneaked away through the woods and up a rocky bluff where he could watch.

Then the big fellow came on Wahb's track and rumbled a deep growl of anger; he followed the trail to the tree, and rearing up, he tore the bark with his claws, far above where Wahb had reached. Then he strode rapidly along Wahb's trail. But the cub had seen enough. He fled back over the Divide into the Meteetsee Canon, and realized in his dim, bearish way that he was at peace there because the Bear-forage was so poor.

As the summer came on, his coat was shed. His skin got very itchy, and he found pleasure in rolling in the mud and scraping his

back against some convenient tree. He never climbed now: his claws were too long, and his arms,though growing big and strong, were losing that suppleness of wrist that makes cub Grizzlies and all Blackbears great climbers. He now dropped naturally into the Bear habit of seeing how high he could reach with his nose on the rubbing-post, whenever he was near one.

He may not have noticed it, yet each time he came to a post, after a week or two away, he could reach higher, for Wahb was growing fast and coming into his strength.

Sometimes he was at one end of the country that he felt was his, and sometimes at another, but he had frequent use for the rubbing-

tree, and thus it was that his range was mapped out by posts with his own mark on them.

One day late in summer he sighted a stranger on his land, a glossy Blackbear, and he felt furious against the interloper. As the Blackbear came nearer Wahb noticed the tan-red face, the white spot on his breast, and then the bit out of his ear, and last of all the wind brought a whiff. There could be no further doubt; it was the very smell: this was the black coward that had chased him down the Piney long ago. But how he had shrunken! Before, he had looked like a giant; now Wahb felt he could crush him with one paw. Revenge is sweet, Wahb felt, though

he did not exactly say it, and he went for that red-nosed Bear. But the Black one went up a small tree like a Squirrel. Wahb tried to follow as the other once followed him, but somehow he could not. He did not seem to know how to take hold now, and after a while he gave it up and went away, although the Blackbear brought him back more than once by coughing in derision. Later on that day, when the Grizzly passed again, the red-nosed one had gone.

As the summer waned, the upper forage-grounds began to give out, and Wahb ventured down to the Lower Meteetsee one night to explore. There was a pleasant odor on the breeze, and following

it up, Wahb came to the carcass of a Steer. A good distance away from it were some tiny Coyotes, mere dwarfs compared with those he remembered. Right by the carcass was another that jumped about in the moonlight in a foolish way. For some strange reason it seemed unable to get away. Wahb's old hatred broke out. He rushed up. In a flash the Coyote bit him several times before, with one blow of that great paw, Wahb smashed him into a limp, furry rag; then broke in all his ribs with a crunch or two of his jaws. Oh, but it was good to feel the hot, bloody juices oozing between his teeth!

The Coyote was caught in a

trap. Wahb hated the smell of the iron, so he went to the other side of the carcass, where it was not so strong, and had eaten but little before clank, and his foot was caught in a Wolf-trap that he had not seen. But he remembered that he had once before been caught and had escaped by squeezing the trap. He set a hind foot on each spring and pressed till the trap opened and released his paw^ About the carcass was the smell that he knew stood for man, so he left it and wandered down-stream; but more and more often he got whiffs of that horrible odor, so he turned and went back to his quiet pinon benches.

THE DAYS OF HIS STRENGTH

'AHB'S third sum-rner had brought him the stature of a large-sized Bear, though not nearly the bulk and power that in time were his. He was very light-colored now, and this was why Spah-wat, a Shoshone Indian who more than once hunted him, called him the Whitebear, or Wahb.

Spahwat was a good hunter, and as soon as he saw the rubbing-tree

on the Upper Meteetsee he knew that he was on the range of a big Grizzly. He bushwhacked the whole valley, and spent many days before he found a chance to shoot; then Wahb got a stinging flesh-wound in the shoulder. Hegrowled horribly, but it had seemed to take the fight out of him; he scrambled up the valley and over the lower hills till he reached a quiet haunt, where he lay down.

His knowledge of healing was wholly instinctive. He licked the wound and all around it, and sought to be quiet. The licking removed the dirt, and by massage reduced the inflammation, and it plastered the hair down as a sort of dressing over the wound to keep out the
air, dirt, and microbes. There could be no better treatment.

But the Indian was on his trail. Before long the smell warned Wahb that a foe was coming, so he quietly climbed farther up the mountain to another resting-place. But again he sensed the Indian's approach, and made off. Several times this happened, and at length there was a second shot and another galling wound. Wahb was furious now. There was nothing that really frightened him but that horrible odor of man, iron, and guns, that he remembered from the day when he lost his Mother; but now all fear of these left him. He heaved painfully up the mountain again, and along under a six-foot

ledge, then up and back to the top of the bank, where he lay flat. On came the Indian, armed with knife and gun; deftly, swiftly keeping on the trail; gloating joyfully over each bloody print that meant such anguish to the hunted Bear. Straight up the slide of broken rock he came, where Wahb, ferocious with pain, was waiting on the ledge. On sneaked the dogged hunter; his eye still scanned the bloody slots or swept the woods ahead, but never was raised to glance above the ledge. And Wahb, as he saw this shape of Death relentless on his track, and smelled the hated smell, poised his bulk at heavy cost upon his quivering, mangled arm, there held until the proper

instant came, then to his sound arm's matchless native force he added all the weight of desperate hate as down he struck one fearful, crushing blow. The Indian sank without a cry, and then dropped out of sight. Wahb rose, and sought again a quiet nook where he might nurse his wounds. Thus he learned that one must fight for peace; for he never saw that Indian again, and he had time to rest and recover.

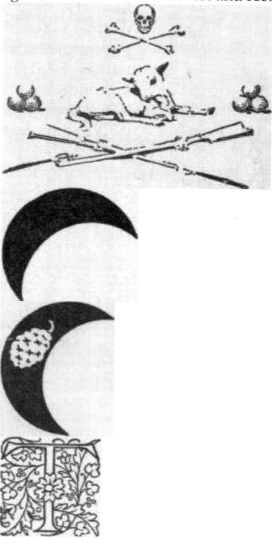

HE years went on as before, except that each winter Wahb slept less soundly, and each spring he came out earlier and was a bigger Grizzly, with fewer enemies that dared to face him. When his sixth year came he was a very big, strong, sullen Bear, with neither friendship nor love in his life since that evil day on the Lower Piney. No one ever heard of Wahb's

mate. No one believes that he ever had one. The love-season of Bears came and went year after year, but left him alone in his prime as he had been in his youth. It is not good for a Bear to be alone; it is bad for him in every way. His habitual moroseness grew with his strength, and any one chancing to meet him now would have called him a dangerous Grizzly.

He had lived in the Meteetsee Valley since first he betook himself there, and his character had been shaped by many little adventures with traps and his wild rivals of the mountains. But there was none of the latter that he now feared, and he knew enough to avoid the first, for that penetrating odor of

man and iron was a never-failing warning, especially after an experience which befell him in his sixth year.

His ever-reliable nose told him that there was a dead Elk down among the timber.

He went up the wind, and there, sure enough, was the great delicious carcass, already torn open at the very best place. True, there was that terrible man-and-iron taint, but it was so slight and the feast so tempting that after circling around and inspecting the carcass from his eight feet of stature, as he stood erect, he went cautiously forward, and at once was caught by his left paw in an enormous Bear-trap. He roared with pain and

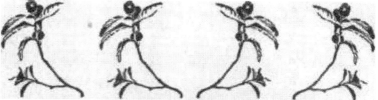

slashed about in a fury. But this was no Beaver-trap; it was a big forty-pound Bear-catcher, and he was surely caught.

Wahb fairly foamed with rage, and madly grit his teeth upon the trap. Then he remembered his former experiences. He placed the trap between his hind legs, with a hind paw on each spring, and pressed down with all his weight. But it was not enough. He dragged off the trap and its clog, and went clanking up the mountain. Again and again he tried to free his foot, but in vain, till he came where a great trunk crossed the trail a few feet from the ground. By chance, or happy thought, he reared again under this and made a new attempt.

With a hind foot on each spring and his mighty shoulders underneath the tree, he bore down with his titanic strength: the great steel springs gave way, the jaws relaxed, and he tore out his foot. So Wahb was free again, though he left behind a great toe which had been nearly severed by the first snap of the steel.

Again Wahb had a painful wound to nurse, and as he was a left-handed Bear, — that is, when he wished to turn a rock over he stood on the right paw and turned with the left, — one result of this disablement was to rob him for a time of all those dainty foods that are found under rocks or logs. The wound healed at last, but he never forgot that experience, and thenceforth the pungent smell of man and iron, even without the gun smell, never failed to enrage him.

Many experiences had taught him that it is better to run if he only smelled the hunter or heard him far away, but to fight desperately if the man was close at hand. And the cowboys soon came to know that the Upper Meteetsee was the range of a Bear that was better let alone.

HI'NE day after a long absence Wahb came into the lower part of his range, and saw to his surprise one of the wooden dens that men make forthemselves. As he came around to get the wind, he sensed the taint that never failed to infuriate him now t and a moment later he heard a loud bang and felt a stinging shock in his left hind leg, the old stiff leg. He wheeled about, in time to see a man running toward the new-made shanty. Had the shot been in his shoulder Wahb would have been helpless, but it was not.

MIGHTY arms that could toss pine logs like broomsticks, paws that with one tap could crush the biggest Bull upon the range, claws that could tear huge slabs of rock from the mountain-side — what was even the deadly rifle to them!

WHEN the man's partner came home that night he found him on the reddened shanty floor. The bloody trail from outside and a shaky, scribbled note on the back of a paper novel told the tale.

It was Wahb done it. I seen him by the spring and wounded him. I tried to git on the shanty, but he ketched me. My God, how I suffer I JACK,

It was all fair. The man had invaded the Bear's country, had .i'« /..^ tried to take the Bear's life, and ; . had lost his own. But Jack's part-/• •' ner swore he would kill that Bear. "* He took up the trail and followed

it up the canon, and there bushwhacked and hunted day after day. He put out baits and traps, and at length one day he heard a crash, clatter, thump, and a huge rock bounded down a bank into a wood, scaring out a couple of deer that floated away like thistle-down. Miller thought at first that it was a land-slide; but he soon knew that it was Wahb that had rolled the boulder over merely for the sake of two or three ants beneath it. The wind had not betrayed him,

so on peering through the bush Miller saw the great Bear as he fed, favoring his left hind leg and growling sullenly to himself at a fresh twinge of pain. Miller steadied himself, and thought, "Here goes a finisher or a dead miss." He gave a sharp whistle, the Bear stopped every move, and, as he stood with ears acock, the man fired at his head.

But at that moment the great shaggy head moved, only an infuriating scratch was given, the smoke betrayed the man's place, and the Grizzly made savage, three-legged haste to catch his foe.

Miller dropped his gun and swung lightly into a tree, the only large one near. Wahb raged in vain against the trunk. He tore off the bark with his teeth and claws; but Miller was safe beyond his reach. For fully four hours the Grizzly watched, then gave it up, and slowly went off into the bushes till lost to view. Miller watched him from the tree, and afterward waited nearly an hour to be sure that the Bear was gone. He then slipped to the ground, got his gun, and set out for camp. But Wahb was cunning; he had only seemed to go away, and then had sneaked back quietly to watch. As soon as the man was away from the tree, too far to return, Wahb dashed after him. In spite of his wounds the Bear could move the faster. Within a quarter of a mile — well,

Wahb did just what the man had sworn to do to him.

Long afterward his friends found the gun and enough to tell the tale.

The claim-shanty on the Me-teetsee fell to pieces. It never again was used, for no man cared to enter a country that had but few allurements to offset its evident curse of ill luck, and where such a terrible Grizzly was always on the war-path.

HEN they found good gold on the Upper Meteetsee. Miners came in pairs and wandered through the peaks, rooting up the ground and spoiling the little streams — grizzly old men mostly, that had lived their lives in the mountain and were themselves slowly turning into Grizzly Bears; digging and grubbing everywhere, not for good, wholesome roots, but

"'AIN'T HE AN AWFUL SIZE, THOUGH?"

for that shiny yellow sand that they could not eat; living the lives of Grizzlies, asking nothing but to be let alone to dig.

They seemed to understand Grizzly Wahb. The first time they met, Wahb reared up on his hind legs, and the wicked green lightnings began to twinkle in his small eyes. The elder man said to his mate:

" Let him alone, and he won't bother you."

" Ain'the an awful size, though ?" replied the other, nervously.

Wahb was about to charge, but something held him back—a something that had no reference to his senses, that was felt only when they were still; a something that

in Bear and Man is wiser than his wisdom, and that points the way at every doubtful fork in the dim and winding trail*

Of course Wahb did not understand what the men said, but he did feel that there was something different here. The smell of man and iron was there, but not of that maddening kind, and he missed the pungent odor that even yet brought back the dark days of his cubhood.

The men did not move, so Wahb rumbled a subterranean growl, dropped down on his four feet, and went on.

Late the same year Wahb ran j across the red-nosed Blackbear.

f How that Bear did keep on shrink-

ing! Wahb could have hurled him across the Graybull with one tap now.

But the Blackbear did not mean to let him try. He hustled his fat, podgy body up a tree at a rate that made him puff. Wahb reached up nine feet from the ground, and with one rake of his huge claws tore off the bark clear to the shining white wood and down nearly to the ground; and the Blackbear shivered and whimpered with terror as the scraping of those awful claws ran up the trunk and up his spine in a way that was horribly suggestive.

What was it that the sight of that Blackbear stirred in Wahb? Was it memories of the Upper

Piney, long forgotten; thoughts of a woodland rich in food?

Wahb left him trembling up there as high as he could get, and without any very clear purpose swung along the upper benches of the Meteetsee down to the Graybull, around the foot of the Rimrock Mountain; on, till hours later he found himself in the timber-tangle of the Lower Piney, and among the berries and ants of the old times.

He had forgotten what a fine land the Piney was: plenty of food, no miners to spoil the streams, no hunters to keep an eye on, and no mosquitos or flies, but plenty of open, sunny glades and sheltering woods, backed up by high, straight cliffs to turn the colder winds.

There were, moreover, no resident Grizzlies, no signs even of passing travelers, and the Black-bears that were in possession did not count.

Wc*hb was well pleased. He rolled his vast bulk in an old Buffalo-wallow, and rearing up against a tree where the Piney Canon quits the Graybull Canon, he left on it his mark fully eight feet from the ground.

In the days that followed he wandered farther and farther up among the rugged spurs of the Shoshones, and took possession as he went. He found the signboards of several Blackbears, and if they were small dead trees he sent them crashing to earth with a drive of his giant paw. If they

were green, he put his own mark over the other mark, and made it clearer by slashing the bark with the great pickaxes that grew on his toes.

The Upper Piney had so long been a Blackbear range that the Squirrels had ceased storing their harvest in hollow trees, and were now using the spaces under flat rocks, where the Blackbears could not get at them; so Wahb found this a land of plenty: every fourth or fifth rock in the pine woods was the roof of a Squirrel or Chipmunk granary, and when he turned it over, if the little owner were there, Wahb did not scruple to flatten him with his paw and devour him as an agreeable relish to his own provisions.

And wherever Wahb went he put up his sign-board:

Trespassers beware!

It was written on the trees as high up as he could reach, and every one that came by understood that the scent of it and the hair in it were those of the great Grizzly Wahb.

If his Mother had lived to train him, Wahb would have known that a good range in spring may be a bad one in summer. Wahb found out by years of experience that a total change with the seasons is best. In the early spring the Cattle and Elk ranges, with their winter-killed carcasses, offer a bountiful feast. In early summer the best forage is on the warm hill-

sides where the quamash and the Indian turnip grow. In late summer the berry-bushes along the river-flat are laden with fruit, and in autumn the pine woods gave good chances to fatten for the winter. So he added to his range each year. He not only cleared out the Blackbears from the Piney and the Meteetsee, but he went over the Divide and killed that old fellow that had once chased him out of the Warhouse Valley. And, more than that, he held what he had won, for he broke up a camp of tenderfeet that were looking for a ranch location on the Middle Meteetsee; he stampeded their horses, and made general smash of the camp. And so all the animals, in-
cluding man, came to know that the whole range from Frank's Peak to the Shoshone spurs was the proper domain of a king well able to defend it, and the name of that king was Meteetsee Wahb.

Any creature whose strength puts him beyond danger of open attack is apt to lose in cunning. Yet Wahb never forgot his early experience with the traps. He made it a rule never to go near that smell of man and iron, and that was the reason that he never again was caught.

So he led his lonely life and slouched around on the mountains, throwing boulders about like pebbles, and huge trunks like matchwood, as he sought for his daily

food. And every beast of hill and plain soon came to know and fly in fear of Wahb, the one time hunted, persecuted Cub. And more than one Blackbear paid with his life for the ill-deed of that other, lorn* ago. And many a cranky Bobcat flying before him took to a tree, and if that tree were dead and dry, Wahb heaved it down, and tree and Cat alike were dashed to bits. Even the proud-necked Stallion, leader of the mustang band, thought well for once to yield the road. The great, grey Timberwolves, and the Mountain Lions too, left their new kill and sneaked in sullen fear aside when Wahb appeared. And if, as he hulked across the sage-covered river-flat sending the scared An-

telope skimming like birds before him, he was faced perchance, by some burly Range-bull, too young to be wise and too big to be afraid, Wahb smashed his skull with one blow of that giant paw, and served him as the Range-cow would have served himself long years ago.

The All-mother never fails to offer to her own, twin cups, one gall, and one of balm. Little or much they may drink, but equally of each. The mountain that is easy to descend must soon be climbed again. The grinding hardship of Wahb's early days, had built his mighty frame. All usual pleasures of a grizzly's life had been denied him but power bestowed in more than double share.

So he lived on year after year, unsoftened by mate or companion, sullen, fearing nothing, ready to fight, but asking only to be let alone — quite alone. He had but one keen pleasure in his sombre life — the lasting glory in his matchless strength — the small but never failing thrill of joy as the foe fell crushed and limp, or the riven boulders grit and heaved when he turned on them the measure of his wondrous force.

EVERYTHING has

a smell of its own for those that have noses to smell. Wahb had been learning smells all his life, and knew the meaning of most of those in the mountains. It was as though each and every thing had a voice of its own for him; and yet it was far better than a voice, for every one knows that a good nose is better than eyes and ears together. And

each of these myriads of voices kept on crying, " Here and such am I."

The juniper-berries, the rosehips, the strawberries, each had a soft, sweet little voice, calling, "Here we are— Berries, Berries/'

The great pine woods had a loud, far-reaching voice, " Here are we, the Pine-trees/' but when he got right up to them Wahb could hear the low, sweet call of the pinon-nuts, " Here are we, the Pinon-nuts."

And the quamash beds in May sang a perfect chorus when the wind was right: "Quamash beds, Quamash beds."

And when he got among them he made out each single voice.

Each root had its own little piece to say to his nose: " Here am I, a big Quamash, rich and ripe/' or a tiny, sharp voice, "Here am I, a good-for-nothing, stringy little root."

And the broad, rich russulas in the autumn called aloud, " I am a fat, wholesome Mushroom," and the deadly amanita cried, " I am an Amanita. Let me alone, or you'll be a sick Bear." And the fairy harebell of the canon-banks sang a song too, as fine as its threadlike stem, and as soft as its dainty blue; but the warden of the smells had learned to report it not, for this, and a million other such, were of no interest to Wahb.

So every living thing that moved,

and every flower that grew, and every rock and stone and shape on earth told out its tale and sang its little story to his nose. Day or night, fog or bright that great, moist nose told him most of the things he needed to know, or passed unnoticed those of no concern, and he depended on it more and more. If his eyes and ears together reported so and so, he would not even then believe it until his nose said, u Yes; that is right."

But this is something that man cannot understand, for he has sold the birthright of his nose for the privilege of living in towns.

While hundreds of smells were agreeable to Wahb, thousands were indifferent to him, a good

many were unpleasant, and some actually put him in a rage.

He had often noticed that if a West wind were blowing when he was at the head of the Piney Canon there was an odd, new scent. Some days he did not mind it, and some days it disgusted him; but he never followed it up. On other days a north wind from the high Divide brought a most awful smell, something unlike any other, a smell that he wanted only to get away from.

WAHB was getting well past his youth now, and he began to have pains in the hind leg that had been wounded so often. After a cold night or a long time of wet weather

he could scarcely use that leg, and one day, while thus crippled, the west wind came down the canon with an odd message to his nose. Wahb could not clearly read the message, but it seemed to say, *Come/ and something within him said, 'Go.' The smell of food will draw a hungry creature and disgust a gorged one. We do not know why, and all that any one can learn is that the desire springs from a need of the body. So Wahb felt drawn by what had long disgusted him, and he slouched up the mountain path,grumbling to himself and slapping savagely back at branches that chanced to switch his face.

The odd odor grew very strong; it led him where he had never been

before — up a bank of whitish sand to a bench of the same color, where there was unhealthy-looking water running down, and a kind of fog coming out of a hole. Wahb threw up his nose suspiciously — such a peculiar smell! He climbed the bench.

A snake wriggled across the sand in front. Wahb crushed it with a blow that made the near trees shiver and sent a balanced boulder toppling down, and he growled a growl that rumbled up the valley like distant thunder. Then he came to the foggy hole. It was full of water that moved gently and steamed. Wahb put in his foot, and found it was quite warm and that it felt pleasantly on his skin. He put in both feet, and little by little went in farther, causing the pool to overflow on all sides, till he was lying at full length in the warm, almost hot, sulphur-spring, and sweltering in the greenish water, while the wind drifted the steam about overhead.

There are plenty of these sulphur-springs in the Rockies, but this chanced to be the only one on Wahb's range. He lay in it for over an hour; then, feeling that he had had enough, he heaved his huge bulk up on the bank, and realized that he was feeling remarkably well and supple. The stiffness of his hind leg was gone.

He shook the water from his shaggy coat. A broad ledge in full

CAUSING THE POOL TO OVERFLOW.

sun-heat invited him to stretch himself out and dry. But first he reared against the nearest tree and left a mark that none could mistake. True, there were plenty of signs of other animals using the sulphur-bath for their ills; but what of it? Thenceforth that tree bore this inscription, in a language of mud, hair, and smell, that every mountain creature could read:

My bath. Keep away
(Signed) WAHB.

Wahb lay on his belly till his back was dry, then turned on his broad back and squirmed about in a ponderous way till the broiling sun had wholly dried him. He

realized that he was really feeling very well now. He did not say to himself, " I am troubled with that unpleasant disease called rheumatism, and sulphur-bath treatment is the thing to cure it." But what he did know was, " I have dreadful pains; I feel better when I am in this stinking pool." So thenceforth he came back whenever the pains began again, and each time he was cured.

THE WANING

'EARS went by. Wahb grew no bigger,—there was no need for that,—but he got whiter, cross-er, and more dangerous. He really had an enormous range now. Each spring, after the winter storms had removed his notice-boards, he went around and renewed them. It was natural to do so, for, first of all, the scarcity of food compelled him to travel all over the range.

There were lots of clay wallows at that season, and the itching of his skin, as the winter coat began to shed, made the dressing of cool, wet clay very pleasant, and the exquisite pain of a good scratching was one of the finest pleasures he knew. So, whatever his motive, the result was the same: the signs were renewed each spring.

At length the Palette Ranch outfit appeared on the Lower Piney, and the men got acquainted with the 'ugly old fellow.' The Cow-punchers, when they saw him, decided they 'had n't lost any Bears and they had better keep out of his way and let him mind his business.'

They did not often see him, although his tracks and sign-boards
were everywhere. But the owner of this outfit, a born hunter, took a keen interest in Wahb. He learned something of the old Bear's history from Colonel Pickett, and found out for himself more than the colonel ever knew.

He learned that Wahb ranged as far south as the Upper Wiggins Fork and north to the Stinking Water, and from the Meteetsee to the Shoshones.

He found that Wahb knew more about Bear-traps than most trappers do; that he either passed them by or tore open the other end of the bait-pen and dragged out the bait without going near the trap, and by accident or design Wahb sometimes sprang the trap with one of
the logs that formed the pen. This ranch-owner found also that Wahb disappeared from his range each year during the heat of the summer, as completely as he did each winter during his sleep.

'ANY years ago a wise government set aside the head waters of the Yellowstone to be a sanctuary of wild life forever. In the limits of this great Wonderland the ideal of the Royal Singer was to be realized, and none were to harm or make afraid. No violence was to be offered to any bird or beast, no ax was to be carried into its primitive forests, and the streams were

to flow on forever unpolluted by mill or mine. All things were to bear witness that such as this was the West before the white man came.

The wild animals quickly found out all this. They soon learned the boundaries of this unfenced Park, and, as every one knows, they show a different nature within its sacred limits. They no longer shun the face of man, they neither fear nor attack him, and they are even more tolerant of one another in this land of refuge.

Peace and plenty are the sum of earthly good; so, finding them here, the wild creatures crowd into the Park from the surrounding country in numbers not elsewhere to be seen.

The Bears are especially numerous about the Fountain Hotel. In the woods, a quarter of a mile away, is a smooth open place where the steward of the hotel has all the broken and waste food put out daily for the Bears, and the man whose work it is has become the Steward of the Bears' Banquet. Each day it is spread, and each year there are more Bears to partake of it. It is a common thing now to see a dozen Bears feasting there at one time. They are of all kinds — Black, Brown, Cinnamon, Grizzly, Silvertip, Roach-backs, big and small, families and rangers, from all parts of the vast surrounding country. All seem to realize that in the Park no violence is allowed, and the most fe-

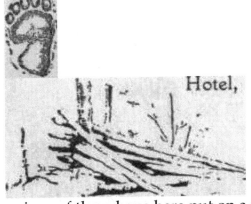

rocious of them have here put on a new behavior. Although scores of Bears roam about this choice resort, and sometimes quarrel among themselves, not one of them has ever yet harmed a man.

Year after year they have come and gone. The passing travellers see them. The men of the hotel know many of them well. They know that they show up each summer during the short season when the hotel is in use, and that they disappear again, no man knowing whence they come or whither they

One day the owner of the Palette Ranch came through the Park. During his stay at the Fountain Hotel, he went to the Bear ban-

quet-hall at high meal-tide. There were several Blackbears feasting, but they made way for a huge Silvertip Grizzly that came about sundown.

"That, 11 said the man who was acting as guide, "is the biggest Grizzly in the Park; but he is a peaceable sort, or Lud knows what r d happen/'

" That! TT said the ranchman, in astonishment, as the Grizzly came hulking nearer, and loomed up like a load of hay among the piney pillars of the Banquet Hall." That! If that is not Meteetsee Wahb, I never saw a Bear in my life! Why, that is the worst Grizzly that ever rolled a log in the Big Horn Basin."

meal-tide. There
ckbears feasting,
way for a huge
that came about

he man who was
"is the biggest
'ark; but he is a
or Lud knows

the ranchman, in
the Grizzly came
nd loomed up like

"It ain't possible/' said the other, "for he T s here every summer, July and August, an' I reckon he don't live so far away."

"Well, that settles it," said the ranchman; "July and August is just the time we miss him on the range; and you can see for yourself that he is a little lame behind and has lost a claw of his left front foot. Now I know where he puts in his summers; but I did not suppose that the old reprobate would know enough to behave himself away from home."

The big Grizzly became very well known during the successive hotel seasons. Once only did he really behave ill, and that was the first season he appeared, before he fully knew the ways of the Park.

He wandered over to the hotel, one day, and in at the front door. In the hall he reared up his eight feet of stature as the guests fled in • terror; then he went into the clerk's office. The man said: " All right; if you need this office more than I do, you can have it," and leaping over the counter, locked himself in the telegraph-off ice, to wire the superintendent of the Park: " Old Grizzly in the office now, seems to want to run hotel; may we shoot?"

The reply came: "No shooting allowed in Park; use the hose." Which they did, and, wholly taken by surprise, the Bear leaped over the counter too, and ambled out the back way, with a heavy thud-thudding of his feet, and a rattling of his claws on the floor. He passed through the kitchen as he went, and, picking up a quarter of beef, took it along.

This was the only time he was known to do ill, though on one occasion he was led into a breach of the peace by another Bear. This was a large she-Blackbear and a noted mischief-maker. She had a wretched, sickly cub that she was very proud of — so proud that she went out of her way to seek trouble on his behalf. And he, like all spoiled children, was the cause of much bad feeling. She was so big and fierce that she fk#, could bully all the other Black-bears, but when she tried to drive off old Wahb she received a pat from his paw that sent her tumbling like a football. He followed her up, and would have killed her, for she had broken the peace of the Park, but she escaped by climbing a tree, from the top of which her miserable little cub was apprehensively squealing at the pitch of his voice. So the affair was ended; in future the Blackbear kept out of Wahb's way, and he won the reputation of being a peaceable, well-behaved Bear. Most persons believed that he came from some remote mountains where were neither guns nor traps to make him sullen and revengeful.

VERY one knows that a Bitter-root Grizzly is a bad Bear. The Bitter-root Range is the roughest part of the mountains. The ground is everywhere cut up with deep ravines and overgrown with dense and tangled underbrush.

It is an impossible country for horses, and difficult for gunners, and there is any amount of good

Bear-pasture. So there are plenty of Bears and plenty of trappers.

The Roachbacks, as the Bitter-root Grizzlies are called, are a cunning and desperate race. An old Roachback knows more about traps than half a dozen ordinary trappers; he knows more about plants and roots than a whole college of botanists. He can tell to a certainty just when and where to find each kind of grub and worm, and he knows by a whiff whether the hunter on his trail a mile away is working with guns, poison, dogs, traps, or all of them together. And he has one general rule, which is an endless puzzle to the hunter: 'Whatever you decide to do, do it quickly and follow it right up.' So

ie hunter:
o do, do it
ht up.' So

when a trapper and a Roachback meet, the Bear at once makes up his mind to run away as hard as he can, or to rush at the man and fight to a finish.

The Grizzlies of the Bad Lands did not do this: they used to stand on their dignity and growl like a thunder-storm, and so gave the hunters a chance to play their deadly lightning; and lightning is wors i than thunder any day. Men can get used to growls that rumble along the ground and up one's legs to ihz little house where one's courage lives; but Bears cannot get used to 45 — 90 soft-nosed bullets, and that is why the Grizzlies of the Bad Lands were all killed off.

So the hunters have learned that they never know what a Roachback will do; but they do know that he is going to be quick about it.

Altogether these Bitter-root Grizzlies have solved very well the problem of life, in spite of white men, and are therefore increasing in their own wild mountains.

Of course a range will hold only so many Bears, and the increase is crowded out; so that when that slim young Bald-faced Roachback found he could not hold the range he wanted, he went out perforce t seek his fortune in the world.

He was not a big Bear, or e would not have been crowded < it;

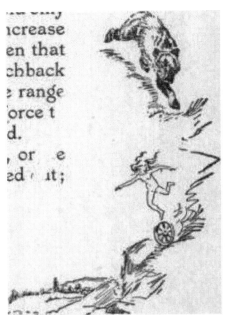

but he had been trained in a good school, so that he was cunning enough to get on very well elsewhere. How he wandered down to the Salmon River Mountains and did not like them; how he traveled till he got among the barb-wire fences of the Snake Plains and of course could not stay there; how a mere chance turned him from going eastward to the Park, where he might have rested; how he made for the Snake River Mountains and found more hunters than berries; how he crossed into the Tetons and looked down with disgust on the teeming man colony of Jackson's Hole, does not belong to this history of Wahb. But when Baldy Roachbackcrossed theGros
    Ventre Range and over the Wind River Divide to the head of the Graybull, he does come into the story, just as he did into the country and the life of the Meteetsee Grizzly.
    The Roachback had not found a man-sign since he left Jackson's Hole, and here he was in a land of plenty of food. He feasted on all the delicacies of the season, and enjoyed the easy, brushless country till he came on one of Wahb's signposts.

"Trespassers beware!" it said in the plainest manner. The Roachback reared up against it.

"Thunder! whataBear!" The nose-mark was a head and neck above Baldy's highest reach. Now,

Baldy jerk
was nothi
over again
had not }
about it;
into his cu

a simple Bear would have gone quietly away after this discovery; but Baldy felt that the mountains owed him a living, and here was a good one if he could keep out of the way of the big fellow. He nosed about the place, kept a sharp lookout for the present owner, and went on feeding wherever he ran across a good thing.

A step or two from this ominous tree was an old pine stump. In the Bitter-roots there are often mice-nests under such stumps, and Baldy jerked it over to see. There was nothing. The stump rolled over against the sign-post. Baldy had not yet made up his mind about it; but a new notion came into his cunning brain. He turned

'HE DELIBERATELY STOOD UP ON THE PINE ROOT.

his head on this side, then on that. He looked at the stump, then at the sign, with his little pig-like eyes. Then he deliberately stood up on the pine root, with his back to the tree, and put his mark away up, a head at least above that of Wahb. He rubbed bis back long and hard, and he sought some mud to smear his head and shoulders, then came back and made the mark so big, so strong, and so high, and emphasized it with such claw-gashes in the bark, that it could be read only in one way — a challenge to the present claimant from some monstrous invader, who was ready, nay anxious, to fight to a finish for this desirable range. Maybe it was accident and may-

be design, but when the Roach -back jumped from the root it rolled to one side. Baldy went on down the canon, keeping the keenest lookout for his enemy.

It was not Ions* before Wahb found the trail of the interloper, and all the ferocity of his outside-the-Park nature was aroused.

He followed the trail for miles on more than one occasion. But the small Bear was quick-footed as well as quick-witted, and never showed himself. He made a point, however, of calling at each signpost, and if there was any means of cheating, so that his mark might be put higher, he did it with a vim, and left a big, showy record. But if there was no chance for any but

a fair register, he would not go near the tree, but looked for a fresh tree near by with some log or side-ledge to reach from.

Thus Wahb soon found the interloper's marks towering far above his own—a monstrous Bear evidently, that even he could not be sure of mastering. But Wahb was no coward. He was ready to fight to a finish any one that might come; and he hunted the range for that invader. Day after day Wahb sought for him and held himself ready to fight. He found his trail daily, and more and more often he found that towering record far above his own. He often smelled him on the wind; but he never saw him, for the old Grizzly's eyes had

grown very dim of late years; things but a little way off were mere blurs to him. The continual menace could not but fill Wahb with uneasiness, for he was not young now, and his teeth and claws were worn and blunted. He was more than ever troubled with pains in his old wounds, and though he could have risen on the spur of the moment to fight any number of Grizzlies of any size, still the continual apprehension, the knowledge that he must hold himself ready at any moment to fight this young monster, weighed on his spirits and began to tell on his general health.

HE Roachback's life was one of continual vigilance, always ready to run, doubling and shifting to avoid the encounterthatmust mean instant death to him. Many a time from some hiding-place he watched the great Bear, and trembled lest the wind should betray him. Several times his very impudence saved him, and more than once he was nearly cornered in a box-

canon. Once he escaped only by climbing up a long crack in a cliff, which Wahb's huge frame could not have entered. But still, in a mad persistence, he kept on marking the trees farther into the range. At last he scented and followed up the sulphur-bath. He did not understand it at all. It had no appeal to him, but hereabouts were the tracks of the owner. In a spirit of mischief the Roachback scratched dirt into the spring, and then seeing the rubbing-tree, he stood sidewise on the rocky ledge, and was thus able to put his mark fully five feet above that of Wahb. Then he nervously jumped down, and was running about, defiling the bath and keeping a sharp lookout,

THE ROACHBACK FLED INTO THE WOODS.

when he heard a noise in the woods below. Instantly he was all alert. The sound drew near, then the wind brought the sure proof, and the Roachback, in terror, turned and fled into the woods.

It was Wahb. He had been failing in health of late; his old pains were on him again, and, as well as his hind leg, had seized his right shoulder, where were still lodged two rifle-balls. He was feeling very ill, and crippled with pain. He came up the familiar bank at a jerky limp, and there caught the odor of the foe; then he saw the track in the mud—his eyes said the track of a small Bear, but his eyes were dim now, and his nose, his unerring nose, said,

"This is the track of the huge invader/' Then he noticed the tree with his sign on it t and there beyond doubt was the stranger's mark far above his own. His eyes and nose were agreed on this; and more, they told him that the foe was close at hand, might at any moment come.

Wahb was feeling ill and weak with pain. He was in no mood for a desperate fight. A battle against such odds would be madness now. So, without taking the treatment, he turned and swung along the bench away from the direction taken by the stranger — the first time since his cubhood that he had declined to fight.

That was a turning-point in Wahb's life. If he had followed up the stranger he would have found the miserable little craven trembling, cowering, in an agony of terror, behind a log in a natural trap, a walled-in glade only fifty yards away, and would surely have crushed him. Had he even taken the bath, his strength and courage would have been renewed, and if not, then at least in time he would have met his foe, and his after life would have been different. But he had turned. This was the fork in the trail, but he had no means of knowing it.

He limped along, skirting the lower spurs of the Shoshones, and soon came on that horrid smell that he had known for years, but

never followed up or understood. It was right in his road, and he traced it to a small, barren ravine that was strewn over with skeletons and dark objects, and Wahb, as he passed, smelled a smell of many different animals, and knew by its quality that they were lying dead in this treeless, grassless hollow. For there was a cleft in the rocks at the upper end, whence poured a deadly gas; invisible but heavy, it filled the little gulch like a brimming poison bowl, and at the lower end there was a steady overflow. But Wahb knew only that the air that poured from it as he passed made him dizzy and sleepy, and repelled him, so that he got quickly away from it and was glad once more to breathe the piny wind.

Once Wahb decided to retreat, it was all too easy to do so next time; and the result worked double disaster. For, since the big stranger was allowed possession of the sulphur-spring, Wahb felt that he would rather not go there. Sometimes when he came across the traces of his foe, a spurt of his old courage would come back. He would rumble that thunder-growl as of old, and go painfully lumbering along the trail to settle the thing right then and there. But he never overtook the mysterious giant, and his rheumatism, growing worse now that he was barred fro'.i the cure, soon made him daily less capable of either running or fight-ing.

Sometimes Wahb would sense his foe f s approach when he was in a bad place for fighting, and, without really running, he would yield to a wish to be on a better footing, where he would have a fair chance. This better footing never led him nearer the enemy, for it is well known that the one awaiting has the advantage.

Some days Wahb felt so ill that it would have been madness to have staked everything on a fight, and when he felt well or a little better, the stranger seemed to keep away.

Wahb soon found that the stranger's track was most often on the Warhouse and the west slope of the Piney, the very best feeding-grounds. To avoid these when he did not feel equal to fighting was

d
only natural, and as he was always in more or less pain now, it amounted to abandoning to the stranger the best part of the range. X *""

Weeks went by. Wahb had meant to go back to his bath, but he never did. His pains grew worse; he was now crippled in his right shoulder as well as in his hind leg. &

The long strain of waiting for the fight begot anxiety, that grew to be apprehension, which, with the sapping of his strength, was ^ breaking down his courage, as it always must when courage is founded on muscular force. His daily care now was not to meet and fight the invader, but to avoid him till he felt better.

Thus that first little retreat grew into one long retreat. Wahb had to go farther and farther down the Piney to avoid an encounter. He was daily worse fed, and as the weeks went by was daily less able to crush a foe.

He was living and hiding at last on the Lower Piney — the very place where once his Mother had Drought him with his little brothers. The life he led now was much like the one he had led after that dark day. Perhaps for the same reason. If he had had a family of his own all might have been different. As he limped along one morning, seeking among the barren aspen groves for a few roots, or the wormy partridge-berries that were too poor

to interest the Squirrel and the Grouse, he heard a stone rattle down the western slope into the woods, and, a little later, on the wind was borne the dreaded taint. He waded through the ice-cold Piney, — oncehe would have leaped it, — and th e ch ill water sent th ro ugh and up each great hairy limb keen pains that seemed to reach his very life. He was retreating again— which way? There seemed but one way now — toward the new ranch-house.

But there were signs of stir about it long before he was near enough to be seen. His nose, his trustiest friend, said, "Turn, turn and seek the hills/' and turn he did even at the risk of meeting there

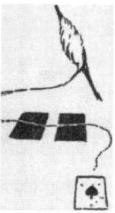

the dreadful foe. He limped painfully along the north bank of the Piney, keeping in the hollows and among the trees. He tried to climb a cliff that of old he had often bounded up at full speed. When half-way up his footing gave way, and down he rolled to the bottom. A long way round was now the only road, for onward he must go — on — on. But where? There seemed no choice now but to abandon the whole range to the terrible stranger. And feeling, as far as a Bear can feel, that he is fallen, defeated, dethroned at last, that he is driven from his ancient range by a Bear too strong for him to face, he turned up the west fork, and the lot was drawn. The strength and speed

were gone from his once mighty limbs; he took three times as long as he once would to mount each well-known ridge, and as he went he glanced backward from time to time to know if he were pursued. Away up the head of the little branch were the Shoshones, bleak, forbidding; no enemies were there, and the Park was beyond it all — on, on he must go. But as he climbed with shaky limbs, and short uncertain steps, the west wind brought the odor of Death Gulch, that fearful little valley where everything was dead, where the very air was deadly. It used to disgust him and drive him away, but now Wahb felt that it had a message for him; he was drawn by it. It was in his

line of flight, and he hobbled slowly toward the place. He went nearer, nearer, until he stood upon the entering ledge. A Vulture that had descended to feed on one of the victims was slowly going to sleep on the untouched carcass. Wahb swung his great grizzled muzzle and his long white beard in the wind. The odor that he once had hated was attractive now. There was a strange biting quality in the air. His body craved it. For it seemed to numb his pain and it promised sleep, as it did that day when first he saw the place.

Far below him, to the right and to the left and on and on as far as the eye could reach, was the great kingdom that once had been his;

where he had lived for years in the glory of his strength; where none had dared to meet him face to face. The whole earth could show no view more beautiful. But Wahb had no thought of its beauty; he only knew that it was a good land to live in; that it had been his, but that now it was gone, for his strength was gone, and he was flying to seek a place where he could rest and be at peace.

Away over the Shoshones, indeed, was the road to the Park, but it was far, far away, with a doubtful end to the long, doubtful journey. But why so far? Here in this little gulch was all he sought; here were peace and painless sleep. He knew it; for his nose, his

never-erring nose, said, "Here! here nowl"

He paused a moment at the gate, and as he stood the wind-borne fumes began their subtle work. Five were the faithful wardens of his life, and the best and trustiest of them all flung open wide the door he long had kept. A moment still Wahb stood in doubt. His lifelong guide was silent now, had given up his post. But another sense he felt within. The Angel of the Wild Things was standing there, beckoning, in the little vale. Wahb did not understand. He had no eyes to see the tear in the Angel's eyes, nor the pitying smile that was surely on his lips. He could not even see the Angel. But he felt him beckoning, beckoning.

"HE PAUSED A MOMENT AT THE GATE.

A rush of his ancient courage surged in the Grizzly's rugged breast. He turned aside into the little gulch. The deadly vapors entered in, filled his huge chest and tingled in his vast, heroic limbs as he calmly lay down on the rocky, herbless floor and as gently went to sleep, as he did that day in his Mother's arms by the Graybull, long ago.

THE END

Made in the USA
San Bernardino, CA
30 April 2018